To:

Lauren

From:

MaaMMAha

9-7-06 ~~7/06~~

Date

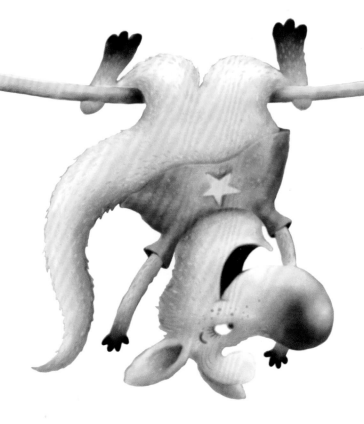

With love to the kids at The Foundry, who inspired this book and changed my life,

~Colleen

To my grandmother Grace, my family, and my friends,

~Paula

Text copyright © 2003 by Colleen Ludington
Illustrations copyright © 2003 by Paula Becker

Published in Nashville, Tennessee, by Tommy Nelson®, a Division of Thomas Nelson, Inc.

Library of Congress Cataloging-in-Publication Data

Ludington, Colleen.
    What I like about you / by Colleen Ludington.
      p. cm.
    Illustrated by Paula Becker.
    Summary: Illustrations and simple rhyming text describe how special and loved a child is as a unique gift from God.
    ISBN 1-4003-0292-7
    1. Individual differences--Religious aspects--Christianity--Juvenile literature. [1. Individuality. 2. Christian life.] I. Becker, Paula, ill.
II. Title.
BV4599.5.I53L83 2003
242'.62--dc21   2003004645

Printed in China

03 04 05 06 07 QWM 5 4 3 2 1

Colleen Ludington

What I Like About You

Illustrated by Paula Becker

Tommy
NELSON
www.tommynelson.com
A Division of Thomas Nelson, Inc.
www.ThomasNelson.com

I could search the world over, from here to Timbuktu,
But I never would find someone else *just like you*.

I could borrow a bloodhound to search and to sniff.

Would he find one like you? No! Not even a whiff.

You're a custom-made kid, by God's own design.

You're not three. You're not two. You are *one* of a kind!

Were you born high in the mountains, overlooking the lakes,
Or down in the bayou with crawdads and snakes?

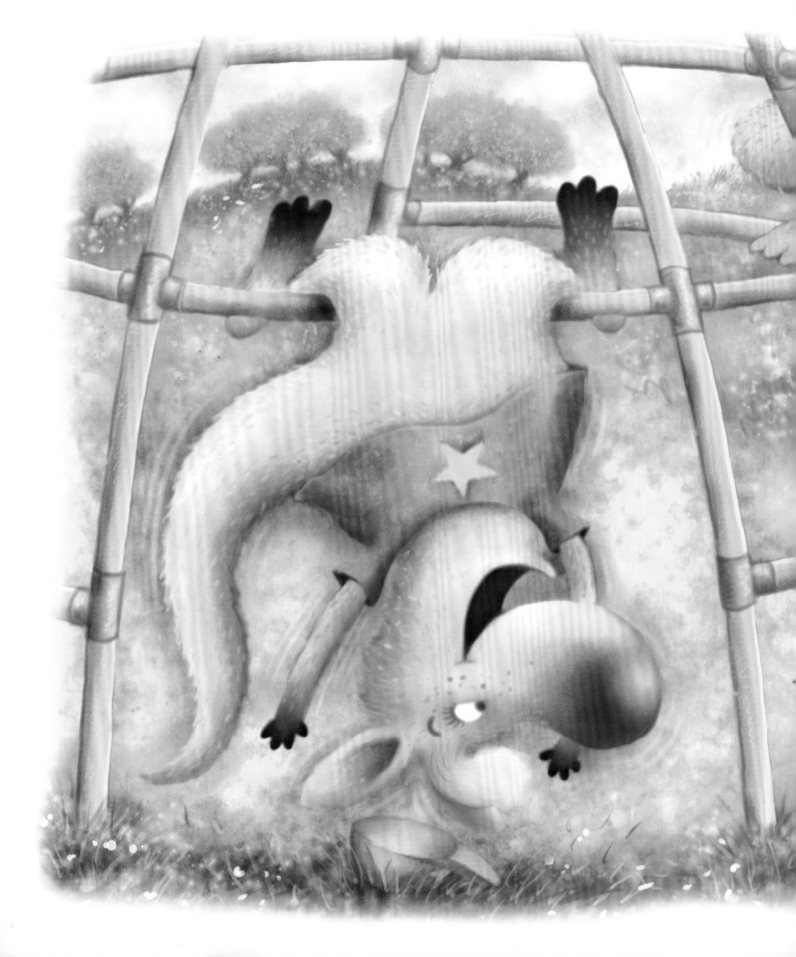

God knows all about you, and He smiled when you came.

He delights in your laugh and the sound of your name.

Curly hair, chubby toes, perfect teeth, freckled nose,

If you're covered with mud or you smell like a rose . . .

Lots of sweet, tiny details make you who you are,

And I celebrate you! You're a real superstar!

From all the "you" things you like to the "you" things you'd change,
There's not one single "you" thing that I'd rearrange.

You're a gift sent to me from God up above,
Perfectly, delightfully created in love.

When I am with you and when we're apart,

You're always here with me—right here in my heart.

I love you completely because you are you—
Not only for the things that you say or you do.

You might snore in your sleep or snort when you laugh;
You might like your sandwiches in triangles or halves.

But you have a purpose no one else can fulfill;

No one can replace you—no one ever will.

Is it all coming clear now? Can you see that it's true?

All those things that I like, are what I LOVE about you!